WELCOME TO DOOM FARMS

BONEGARDEN #1

KARSTEN KNIGHT

WELCOME TO DOOM FARMS

Bonegarden #1

Copyright © 2018 by Karsten Knight

www.karstenknightbooks.com

First edition: September 2018

PROLOGUE

I raced my bike through the dark orchard, fleeing for my life.

My whole body vibrated as the tires rumbled over the uneven ground. In the dense fog, it felt like the apple trees were closing in around me. One appeared through the mist right in my path, and I swerved sharply to avoid it.

My front tire snagged on a gnarled root. Next thing I knew, I was somersaulting over the handlebars.

I landed flat on my back, sending a cluster of rotting apples scattering around me like marbles. The air exploded out of my lungs. The bike flipped end over end beside me, nearly crushing my head in the process.

Somehow, through the dull ache in my back, I sucked in a deep breath and mustered the will to stand up. I abandoned the bike to finish the journey to the waterfall on foot.

There were only two choices now:

Run or die.

The creature would find me in less than a minute.

By the time I reached the river, my lungs burned for air. I limped out onto the floating wooden platform, feeling it sway from the raging rapids below. The waterfall roared beneath me. One wrong step and the river would carry me right over the edge, to plummet a hundred feet to my death.

But what was waiting for me back the way that I came was so much more terrifying.

Before me, a giant jack-o'-lantern grinned menacingly. Flames danced in its eyes. *Abandon all hope*, it seemed to be saying to me. *There is no escaping the beast.*

It was true. I had reached a dead end. I huddled in front of the pumpkin, shivering as the cold mist settled on my skin. I stared into the dark.

Over the deafening rush of water, I heard something else, a noise that made my stomach knot with dread.

The *click-click-click* of long, spindly legs, marching toward me.

Through the dark fog, I watched the creature's glowing sapphire eyes appear.

As its razor-sharp tail glinted above me, preparing to strike, I had only one thought:

I wish I could go back in time to stop myself from ever planting those seeds.

I

FOUR WEEKS EARLIER

I t was official: my parents were trying to kill me.

That was the only way I could explain why they made me, Kayla Dunn, pack up just three weeks into fifth grade and leave all my friends behind.

I was a city kid, used to the bustle and excitement of living in downtown Boston. Back in the city, I could walk to the movie theater, catch a Red Sox game after school, or choose from a thousand different restaurants for dinner.

Now here I was, in the back of our station wagon as it rattled through the countryside down a shady, tree-lined road. No malls, no baseball stadiums, none of my best friends. Instead of the skyscrapers I grew up around, there was only flat farmland as far as the eye could see.

I had given up counting cows and horses miles ago. They outnumbered the humans here twenty to one.

"We're almost home!" Mom exclaimed from the front seat. "Didn't I tell you that Orchard Falls would be beautiful, Kayla?"

I couldn't disagree with her there. It was late September and the foliage had begun to turn the colors of sunset. A billboard advertised Orchard Falls as "Home of the world-famous Jack-o'-Lantern Festival." In fact, the town was so crazy about pumpkins that they had even painted their water tower orange to resemble one. Its wicked grin leered down at us as we passed it.

As we drove over a creek through an old covered bridge, I realized that Orchard Falls really *was* like a town straight out of a movie.

Maybe I could learn to enjoy living here after all.

"The Jack-o'-Lantern Festival is one of the biggest country fairs in the state!" Dad explained from the driver's seat. "In just a couple of weeks, you'll be able to take a hay ride, and bob for apples, and compete in the pie-eating contest until you puke!"

"Gross, Dad," I said, but I smiled. This was my father's hometown. He had dreamed of moving back here for a long time. I was still surprised when my parents sat me down and told me their plan: to give up their jobs in the city and buy a farm out here. The two of them had always struggled just to keep house-plants alive. I had no idea how they would manage an entire field of crops.

The backseat of the car was littered with books about growing every fruit and vegetable imaginable—corn, watermelon, a small vineyard for grapes. Even now, my mom was rambling about how she wanted to launch her own line of homemade jams using recipes that had been passed down from my grandfather. For the hundredth time, she repeated her cheesy sales pitch: "Your toast isn't *Dunn* until you spread it with Dunn Farms Jams!"

"It's un-*Dunn*-iably delicious!" Dad added.

I groaned. "I think I'm *Dunn* listening to both of your puns."

As we rounded the final curve in the road, Dad said, "I have a special surprise for the two of you. Before I left, I ordered a big new sign to advertise the farm. I think it's really going to catch the eye of potential customers!" He squinted out the window and drummed his hands dramatically on the steering wheel. "It should be visible as soon as we pass this last line of apple trees, in 3 ... 2 ... 1 ..."

The station wagon popped out past the last tree. Sure enough, a big sign greeted anyone who drove past the property. All three of us frowned up at it.

Someone had misspelled our last name.

In big letters, the sign read:

Welcome to Doom Farms.

2

I was the first to speak as we gawked up at the unfortunate billboard. "Well, you weren't kidding when you said it would catch people's attention," I said.

Dad scowled. "We've only been in town for five minutes, and already we have to deal with vandalism?"

As I peered closer, I realized the sign *had* originally spelled Dunn correctly, but someone had spray painted over the last three letters.

"Doom Farm Jams," I pronounced in my best television commercial voice. "They're so delicious you'll just die."

Mom tried to glare at me in the rearview mirror, but soon all three of us were laughing. "Oh well," she said. "A little prank by some local kids isn't going to ruin this great day."

"That's the spirit!" Dad cried. He shifted the station wagon back into drive and continued past the sign. "Although I bet the culprit was my childhood nemesis, Ezekiel Slade. He still owns a farm down the street. I bet this was his 'welcome to the neighborhood' gift. We'll see who gets the last laugh when our pumpkins win best in show at the Jack-o'-Lantern Festival."

"Yes, dear," my mom replied sarcastically. "You'll sure show him." She winked at me and reached back for a high-five between the seats.

The car approached our new house, a rustic red farm with white shutters. Half the paint had peeled and fallen away. The house was so old that I worried a strong breeze might make the whole building cave in.

A rickety wooden barn loomed off to the side, along with a metal silo, which I had read was a structure that farmers use to store grain. It looked like a towering aluminum can that a giant had discarded in the field.

Before Dad had even fully parked in the driveway, I jumped out of the moving station wagon and hit the ground running, grateful to be free after the endless ride. Most kids would have bee-lined straight inside to check out their new room, but I had a different destination:

The pumpkin patch.

Halloween is my favorite holiday. There is nothing I love more than carving jack-o'-lanterns—I actually won awards for it at my old school the past few years. Mom and Dad promised me that if we moved to the farm, they would let me take charge of the pumpkin patch. Ordinarily, I wasn't crazy about doing chores, but this job actually sounded like fun.

So when I rounded the corner of the house and stepped into the backyard, I was immediately horrified by what I saw.

The patch lay at the edge of the cornfield, and it was a complete disaster!

The pumpkin vines had all withered and died. Their leaves had turned an ugly shade of brown. Only a few scrawny pumpkins remained.

I had to chase away a crow to stop it from tearing one of the pumpkins apart with its beak. Through the hole it had pecked, I could see a cluster of wriggling maggots eating away at the rotten insides.

It was the grossest thing I had ever seen.

I sighed and sat down on a nearby stump, already feeling defeated. Ahead of me, I noticed that a scarecrow with a pumpkin for a head perched at the edge of the cornfield. Hay poked out of its flannel shirt and jeans.

"Thanks for nothing," I muttered at it, kicking the pumpkin the bird had ripped apart. "Some scarecrow you are."

That's when the scarecrow turned its head to stare at me.

3

I gasped and fell off the stump, landing directly on a rotting pumpkin. The scarecrow groaned. It freed itself from its wooden post and dropped heavily to the ground.

I started to scramble backwards, but the scarecrow lumbered in my direction. One step. Two steps. Dried cornhusks crackled under its feet.

Its jack-o'-lantern grin leered down at me. Its triangular eyes were menacing and cold, two pools of darkness staring out from holes in the orange rind.

As it loomed over me, it lifted its gloved hands. It wrapped them around the pumpkin—and ripped its own head right off!

I released a short-lived scream but stopped when I saw what was left on top of the scarecrow's shoulders.

A boy about my age laughed hysterically. Pumpkin pulp coated his hay-colored hair. "You should have seen the look on your face!" he said. "Priceless!"

My heart thudded against my ribcage. "You jerk!" I snapped. "What was that for?"

He shrugged. "That's just how we greet people around here." He extended his hand to help me up.

Grudgingly, I let him pull me back to my feet. He burst into laughter all over again once he saw the seat of my pants. The pumpkin had exploded when I fell on it, smearing the butt of my jeans in rotten, gooey pulp. Sickening.

"I'm Charlie Slade," he said after he finally composed himself. "I live on the farm next door."

The name Slade rang a bell. He must be the son of my father's old rival, Ezekiel. "Kayla Dunn," I replied. I tried my best to crush his hand in my grip as I shook it. "How long were you waiting up on that post?"

Charlie stretched out his back until it cracked. "Over an hour. It was totally worth it, though."

I gazed across the sprawling field that was now my backyard. It had seen better days. The cornstalks had withered to dry brown husks, and the grapes in the vineyard had shriveled to raisins under the hot sun.

I sighed. Some farm this turned out to be. "So what is there to do for fun around here when you're not pretending to be a scarecrow or terrorizing your neighbors?" I asked.

"Well, the big Jack-o'-Lantern Festival is coming up in just a few weeks," Charlie said. "My family always wins the big prize for best pumpkin in show each year. That trophy has the Slade family name engraved all over it!" He smirked at the devastated ruins of my farm's pumpkin patch. "But I'm *real* scared that you're going to beat us this year. Too bad there's no prize for the pumpkin with the most maggots."

I crossed my arms. "We'll see about that. A lot can happen in a few weeks."

"Yeah, it's plenty of time … for you to get a life!" Charlie cackled and ruffled my hair, then started wandering toward the edge of the farm. "Welcome to the neighborhood, *Kayla Doom*."

I scowled at him as he disappeared into the dark forest that surrounded our property. Between frightening me with the scarecrow prank and mocking me now, Charlie Slade had declared war.

I picked up the jack-o'-lantern head he had

discarded, a healthy, round pumpkin that had obviously come from the Slade farm, not ours. If I really wanted to show up Charlie and put him in his place, I had only one choice:

I had to grow a pumpkin that could beat his at the country fair.

4

That evening, we had our first dinner at the new farm. Before we moved, my dad had talked a big game about eating food grown right on our land. Eggplant parmigiana, fresh watermelon salad, rhubarb pie—he had an entire binder of recipes he had collected before the move.

Instead, we had to order a pizza, since the crops were too rotten to even toss a salad together. I was excited to start unpacking, so I wolfed down two slices and excused myself, taking a can of cola to go.

My new room was on the second floor of the old farmhouse. It had a musty odor that clung to the antique wallpaper, and I kept sneezing from all the dust. The warped floorboards creaked loudly even if I tiptoed across them.

Mom said that once we got a rug and some art to hang on the walls, it would feel more like home.

I wasn't so sure about that.

Even though my room was old and weird, I did like one thing: it had a large picture window that overlooked the fields out back. I imagined a day soon when I could wake up each morning and gaze out over my pumpkin patch, deciding which gigantic gourd to enter into the festival. Maybe I would name each one.

I fell asleep early that night, exhausted from the long day of driving and unpacking. I had weird, vivid nightmares in which the farmhouse itself came alive and tried to devour me. When I finally fled out into the cornfield, I found a whole army of scarecrows waiting for me—not one, but twenty of them. They surrounded me, reaching out for me with their hay-stuffed arms. One of them closed two gloved hands around my neck. "Welcome to Doom Farms, Kayla …" he growled.

I woke up with a sharp gasp. Sweat had matted my hair against my forehead, and the damp sheets had become tangled around me.

My room was still dark. The only light came from the alarm clock, which read just after 2 a.m. I thought at first that it had just been the bad dreams that woke me up in the dead of night.

Then I heard something raking at my window.

I crept toward the glass, afraid of what I might find. Who knew what kind of creatures came out of the forest at night! I had no idea what kind of animal could climb up to the second floor.

I let out a sigh of relief—the noise had just been the shutters clattering against the window. A fierce wind howled outside, rustling the dry cornstalks out back. The whole field rippled as though it were alive.

When I turned my gaze to the pumpkin patch, I saw a dark shape moving around. At first, I thought it was Charlie, back to play another prank on me or sabotage our crops.

As my eyes adjusted to the low light, however, I realized the shadowy man was too tall to be Charlie. He wore a long black cloak and a wide-brimmed hat.

Then he turned his head to stare right at my window.

I gasped and ducked down. Had the stranger seen me? When I worked up the courage to peek back over the windowsill, I expected him to be slowly stalking toward the house.

But the dark figure had not moved. I realized with relief that I wasn't what had captured his attention.

He was gazing up at the full moon, as if he were absorbing energy from the pale light. His cloak billowed around him in the wind.

After a minute, he knelt down in the pumpkin patch. I couldn't see what he was doing from this far away, so I grabbed my phone off the nightstand. I turned on the camera, zoomed in on the stranger, and squinted at the screen.

In one hand, he held a glass test tube. With the other, he scooped up a clump of dirt and sprinkled it into the container. He put a cork in that tube and withdrew another from his cloak.

This time, I watched him dig deeper into the earth, until his arm disappeared all the way up to the elbow. After fishing around in the soil, he pulled out a giant, wriggling worm between two fingers. I clamped a hand over my mouth and gagged in disgust as he dropped the slimy creature into the tube.

While he continued to take more samples, I zoomed in on his face to get a better look. The wide brim of his hat cast a shadow over his features.

I decided to take a picture so I would have proof of this trespassing weirdo.

Only I didn't realize until too late that I had left the flash on.

The man jerked his head up as the bright light

illuminated the field. I gasped but didn't move from the sill.

Instead of fleeing, the trespasser stared up at my window for what felt like forever. I held my breath the entire time.

Then the stranger casually clipped the last tube to his belt, turned, and walked into the cornstalks until they swallowed him up.

I shuddered. At least I had a photo of him now that I could show my parents, or even the police if necessary. I hoped that the flash had been bright enough to light up his face under that hat.

Except when I looked down at my phone, the image only showed the barren pumpkin patch and the cornfield beyond it.

The man wasn't in the picture at all.

5

The next morning, the memory of the stranger seemed like a bizarre nightmare. When I went out to the pumpkin patch, I found a trail of boot prints too large to belong to me or even that nosy Charlie Slade.

It had all been real.

At breakfast, I told my dad what had happened. He stopped flipping pancakes when I mentioned the man in the dark hat. I figured that he would instantly want to call the police, or buy attack dogs, or install an electrified fence around the perimeter.

Instead, his face scrunched up into a furious scowl. "It must have been that jerk, Ezekiel Slade. He was always taller than the rest of our class. First he vandalizes our sign, and now our crops?" He sighed. "Not that there's much left out there to vandalize."

Could it be true? Could the man I saw last night be Charlie's father? Maybe scaring my brains out in my own backyard ran in their family.

Well, if that was the case, then I would get my revenge on both of them when my pumpkins beat theirs at the country fair!

If I wanted to even have a chance of being ready in time, one thing was clear: I needed to start my patch *today*.

After devouring a full stack of my dad's signature butterscotch pancakes, I rode my bike into town. Dad suggested that I check out the giant waterfall that had given Orchard Falls its name. "Just don't get too close to the edge!" he cautioned me.

Although I had been sad to leave my friends in the city, I had to admit that it was more relaxing out here in the country—nothing but miles of cornfields and farmland, and no traffic in sight.

My dad's directions led me down the main road through the town's sprawling apple orchards. When I reached the creek, I followed the path along its banks, heading south. The farther I traveled, the more intense the river grew. It eventually transformed from a serene trickle into raging rapids.

I heard the roar of the waterfall before I even saw it. As I biked closer, I watched the river crash over a series of jagged stones that looked like broken teeth. After that, the water abruptly disappeared over the edge of a cliff.

I had always been afraid of heights. One night back in the city, my parents had taken me to a restaurant on the top floor of a skyscraper. I nearly threw up my dinner every time I made the mistake of gazing out the window.

I nervously moved toward the safety railing that protected the cliff's edge. "Country Kayla is braver than City Kayla," I told myself. "New town, new you." With a deep breath, I finally mustered up the courage to peek over the railing.

Big mistake. I immediately felt dizzy, mesmerized by the sight of the thunderous falls plummeting to the basin a hundred feet below. The water landed so hard that some of it instantly turned into mist and drifted off through the valley.

I swallowed and stepped away from the edge. I had to close my eyes until the dizziness stopped. *You're safe now*, I reminded myself.

If only I knew just how wrong I would turn out to be.

6

Now that I had seen the town's signature landmark—and faced my fears in the process —shopping for pumpkin seeds sounded like a tame, stress-free task. To my dismay, nothing was open when I arrived at the pathetic strip of storefronts that Orchard Falls laughably called "downtown." The general store, the flower shop, the town's only diner, which was the size of our garage—all closed because it was Sunday.

I was about to give up when I came upon a chalkboard sign just outside of town. "Seed Sale!" it read. An arrow pointed down an unpaved road.

I followed the path until I came to a rickety shack. Tall weeds grew wild around it, and the shop was silent except for the chirp of crickets out in the field.

I stepped onto the porch. A swing rocked even though there was no breeze, as though someone had just gotten off it.

It was hard to imagine that this little shack could be a real store, but a handwritten sign in the window cheerfully declared, "Come in!" so I shrugged and opened the screen door.

The store was dark except for a few slivers of daylight shining through the grungy windowpanes. Shelves lined the cramped space, forming a maze. As far as I could see, there were no other customers— and no shopkeeper, either, for that matter.

"Hello?" I called out. "I'm just here to buy some seeds for my pumpkin patch. Hello?"

I stopped talking when I noticed the glass jar on the shelf in front of me. Murky water swirled about inside. I picked it up off the shelf. As I peered through the glass, a dark figure slowly rotated into view.

A black exoskeleton.

A long, curled tail that ended in a stinger.

Two powerful sets of claws.

I stared into the dead scorpion's four pairs of glassy eyes, and wrinkled my face in disgust. The rest of the jars on this shelf contained a series of other creatures. A python. A jellyfish. A horseshoe crab.

What kind of creepy farm supply store kept the carcasses of dead animals on display?

I went to put the jar back on the shelf—

And found a man gazing through the gap right back at me.

I shrieked, so startled that I dropped the jar. It shattered all over the floor. Cold, foul-smelling liquid splattered against my shoes and socks.

"I didn't mean to scare you," the man said in a raspy but quiet voice. He bowed his pale head. "My apologies."

He stepped around the shelf and I instantly felt embarrassed for screaming. The tall man wore denim overalls, leather gardening gloves, and a name tag that identified him as "Abel."

He was clearly just the shopkeeper.

In fact, the man didn't look that scary at all up close. He was probably my father's age, though his skin was so smooth that he could have been younger. His graying hair was cropped shorter than his neatly trimmed beard. He must have worn colored contacts because his eyes were an unnaturally vivid shade of orange, like two marbles plucked from the fire.

I realized I had just been staring in stunned silence. This guy probably thought I was a total freak show for breaking his jar.

"I'm the one who's sorry," I said, pointing down at the mess of broken glass and the fluid soaking into the dusty floorboards.

"Forget about it." The man poked at the scorpion's carcass with the toe of his boot. "It's not like it can die a second time. What can I do for you today?"

I took a deep breath and explained everything— moving to Orchard Falls, the rotting pumpkin patch, the competition coming up in a few weeks.

"I know that if I want to grow a pumpkin big enough to have a chance at the festival, it could take months," I finished. "But if you have something that might even give me a head start, I'm willing to try." *I will do anything to keep Charlie from making a mockery of my new home*, I added silently.

I expected Abel to laugh in my face. Instead, he tapped his chin thoughtfully for a few moments. "I might have something of interest to you," he said. A smile spread across his thin lips. "Please follow me."

W hen Abel threw open the shack's back door, a gust of hot, humid air instantly enveloped me. The hairs on the back of my neck stood upright as I passed over the threshold.

I stepped out into a greenhouse filled with strange plants and flowers. Ivy crisscrossed the foggy windows. The sunlight took on an emerald tint as it filtered through the glass.

As I passed down a row of specimens, I discovered that these were no ordinary plants:

A cactus with spines that oozed droplets of golden liquid.

A large Venus flytrap with a sticky layer of half-digested bugs.

An orchid with petals that camouflaged with the scenery behind it when I approached.

"Are these … natural?" I asked.

"Natural?" Abel echoed. He stepped in front of the Venus flytrap. Maybe it was a trick of the light, but the plant seemed to lean toward him. He delicately ran a finger along the flytrap's thorny teeth, and its jaws opened wider. "The world is full of organisms with extraordinary gifts. Sometimes they develop these talents on their own. Other times they just need a little push."

He pulled a flask from one of the pockets in his overalls and tapped a few drops of what looked like blood into the flytrap's open mouth.

When the drops landed inside, its jaws snapped shut.

"For instance …" Abel continued, striding over to the cluster of bamboo next to me. The green stalks had grown so tall they seemed ready to burst through the glass overhead. "Some bamboo species can grow three feet per day. A pumpkin plant, on the other hand, takes three to four months before it matures. What if the pumpkin could learn something from the bamboo?"

"Maybe the bamboo should teach a class," I joked. "Get tall in thirty days or your money back!"

Abel stared at me blankly. "Bamboo can't talk," he said matter-of-factly. "Its stem lacks a mouth."

Tough crowd, I thought. What a weird dude.

He led me over to a small lab bench covered in diagrams of various plants and animals. The one on top showed a dissected tentacle from an octopus, with notes scribbled next to its suction cups.

Before I could see more, Abel swept the drawings off the table with his arm. They fluttered to the floor, revealing a small chest. Abel unlatched the clasp and flipped open the top.

I leaned in to get a closer look at the red velvet-lined interior. The box was empty except for four pumpkin seeds, each delicately placed side by side. Instead of the normal white color, these seeds were a deep shade of blue.

Maybe it was a trick of the light, but they appeared to emit a faint glow, as if they were radioactive.

"I bred these seeds myself," Abel said, a swell of pride in his voice. "If they don't grow in your fields, then I don't know what will."

"Only four of them?" I asked. I couldn't hide my disappointment. I imagined that Slade Farms must have a sea of pumpkins.

Abel chuckled. "These pumpkins get monstrously

big. I think even with four you'll find you have your hands full soon enough …"

When he said the word "soon," I made up my mind: I needed those seeds at any cost. I pulled a wad of money from my jeans, everything I had saved up from babysitting over the summer back in the city. "How much?" I asked.

Abel waved my money away. "Consider these a free trial," he replied. "If you're happy with the results, come back and see me again. By then, I'll have even better specimens for you."

I couldn't believe my luck. "Thank you," I stammered finally. "I was starting to think this town was full of jerks."

Abel smiled, closed the lid of the chest, and handed it to me. "Well, like you, I'm not originally from around here."

Before I left, Abel gave me a detailed list of instructions for caring for the plants. It explained how far apart to plant them and how often to water them. He even included tubes of special fertilizer that he promised would accelerate their growth.

After I had thanked him profusely, I climbed back onto my bike out front and placed the pumpkin seed chest in the basket over my handlebars. I called out a final "Thank you!" as I pedaled away down the lane.

Abel stood on the front porch, waving a slow goodbye. I heard his soft voice say, "See you soon, Kayla Dunn."

It didn't occur to me at the time that I had never told him my name.

9

T he moment I got home, I headed directly for the old barn. The red doors creaked in protest as I pulled them open.

The stale smell of manure and moldy hay washed over me. How long had it been since the barn had been aired out? It reeked worse than my musty bedroom.

The inside of the barn was like a museum of farming equipment. A tractor that probably hadn't been driven in years sat neglected in the corner. Rows of shovels and pitchforks lined the walls, gathering rust. A massive hay bale dangled from a hook in the ceiling, and I made sure to avoid walking underneath it. It would be hard to grow pumpkins if I was a pancake.

It was a shame the barn smelled so bad. The lofts up top would have made an excellent place for a sleepover or a game of hide and seek.

I eventually found the items I was looking for: a garden trowel for digging and a watering can so dented it looked like a group of kids had played soccer with it.

On my way back past the house, my mother popped her head out of the kitchen window. "Hey, honey!" she called. "The neighbors sent over some of their boysenberries and I'm experimenting with a new jam recipe. Want to be my assistant? I'll let you stir the pot and be my official taste tester!"

I caught a whiff of something tart and fruity through the window. My stomach growled from hunger.

However, I was on a mission and refused to be distracted. "Maybe later," I told her. "These pump-kins aren't going to plant themselves!"

Mom laughed. "Okay, just don't wear yourself out too much. Even the best farmers take snack breaks. And don't forget, your first day of school is tomorrow."

Ugh. Like I needed reminding. I had always liked going to school well enough, but the thought of showing up for class in a small town where everyone already knew each other sounded like an absolute nightmare.

I followed Abel's instructions to the letter, using the garden trowel to build three small mounds. All together they formed a giant triangle.

I planted one seed in each of the little hills, making a hole with the trowel's handle. I took the fourth seed, which was larger than the others, and planted a fourth mound in the center.

Then I filled up the watering can with the hose and soaked the entire patch until the soil turned dark brown. Back at the store, Abel had told me not to worry about overwatering them. "For these pumpkins to grow to their full potential, they're going to need a *lot* of water—gallons of it every day. I bred them to be extra thirsty."

For the finishing touch, I sprinkled each plant with a few droplets of the special fertilizer Abel gave me. It looked like cough syrup, thick and red, as it dripped from the vial.

When I was done, I stepped back and admired my work. The pyramid design of the mounds looked like some sort of ritualistic symbol had been carved into the earth.

The next part would be the hardest:

Waiting.

10

I woke up the next morning to the sound of my mother bursting into my bedroom. She sang the words "First day of school!" repeatedly in a melody she made up as she went along. She dramatically threw open the curtains, but I have no idea why, since it was so early there was no daylight to be found.

I groaned and blinked the sleep from my eyes. I wasn't sure what was worse: that the sun hadn't even risen yet or that my mom couldn't sing on pitch to save her life.

I grudgingly rolled out of bed and dressed in jeans and a t-shirt. Everyone in my old school in the city had been obsessed with fashion, but I didn't want to be branded a snob on my first day here. It was kind of a relief that I might not be judged anymore for being behind on the latest trends. Even kinder-garteners in the city were wearing designer clothes these days!

After eating some of my mom's jam biscuits, I wandered out to the pumpkin patch. Ordinary seeds could take a full week to sprout, but I clung to hope that something might have happened overnight.

I sighed. They were still just mounds of dirt, without so much as a speck of green in sight. Maybe that quack had sold me regular seeds. Heck, they could have been seed-shaped rocks for all I knew.

The sun had finally risen by the time I biked to school. I felt anxious walking into the building, but the secretaries were so nice in the front office that I felt my nerves ease immediately.

"Here you go, darlin'," the redheaded office manager said with a thick twang. She handed me a class schedule and a slip with my locker combination. She glanced around to make sure no one was watch-ing, then pulled a candy bar from her desk drawer and added it to my pile. "A little chocolate always gets me through the tough days," she said with a wink.

As I navigated the halls to my locker, my mouth full of chocolate, I thought that maybe the first day of school wouldn't be so bad after all. Maybe a fresh start was exactly what I needed. Most of the students

I passed gave me friendly smiles or waved. People in the city never even made eye contact with strangers.

I was still grinning when I spun my locker's dial to the combination on my slip: 38 - 17 - 24.

Then I opened the door and was immediately hit in the face with a tidal wave of ooze.

11

I shrieked and staggered back, clawing at the foul-smelling goo that now coated my face. When I cleared my eyes and held up my hands, I saw orange pulp and white seeds.

Someone had rigged my locker to spray pumpkin pulp at me when I opened it.

On cue, I heard someone laughing. Most of the students had already gone to homeroom. The few that remained gawked at my gunk-covered cheeks and clothes.

Tall, gangly Charlie Slade stood to the side, laughing so hard he was clutching his stomach.

"Don't worry," he said between guffaws. "That's fresh pumpkin from *my* farm. I wasn't coldhearted enough to use the rotting pulp from *your* pathetic fields."

My first instinct was to cry. I could already feel the tears welling in my eyes. The pulp was soaking into my hair. I would be lucky if it didn't dye my bangs tangerine.

I looked around at the other students who were still staring at me, waiting for me to react. Whatever I did now would be their first impression of me for years to come.

So I blinked back the tears. I walked calmly over to Charlie. I ran my fingers through my hair, until I had collected an entire handful of pulp.

Then I smeared it across the front of Charlie's denim overalls.

A loud "oooooohhhh" echoed from the crowd around us.

Charlie's mouth hung open. Speechless, he looked at the trail of pulp across his chest and he balled his hands into fists.

"That was a waste of perfectly good pumpkin," I told him. "Next time just bake me a pie."

The hall erupted in laughter and applause. Charlie's cheeks turned a bright shade of red.

He leaned down and wagged a finger in my face.

"This isn't over, Kayla *Dung*." Then he stormed off down the hallway and out of sight.

An African American girl walked up and high-fived me. "Charlie Slade has had that coming for a long time, so thank you for that," she said. "I'm Yvonne, by the way."

I shook her hand. "Kayla," I said.

Yvonne took the schedule from my hands and examined it. "Looks like we have the same first-period biology class. I'll walk you there." She took a second look at my face and cringed. "On second thought, let's stop by the bathroom and try to get you cleaned up first. Cool?"

I nodded and followed her. "I wouldn't want to look like a pumpkin monster on the first day of class!"

12

I left school that day with a new friend, a grin on my face, and a pile of books from the library on proper pumpkin care. I needed all the help I could get if I wanted to crush Charlie's dreams at the big fair.

The day only got better when I came home to a miracle.

I filled up the dented watering can and walked dutifully out to the pumpkin patch. I refused to give up just because the seeds were not the magical variety I thought they were.

What I saw made me stop in my tracks.

Green. Lots of green.

Somehow, during the six hours I had spent in class, the seeds had sprouted. These weren't just tiny shoots emerging from the ground, either. Vines had already started to form, erupting with broad leaves bigger than my hands. I touched one of the tendrils in wonder.

Abel hadn't been lying about these plants growing quickly.

As I circled the patch, I found an intruder. A rabbit was nibbling on one of the pumpkin buds. I knew from the gardening books I had been reading that the pumpkins eventually grew out of the female flowers. The last thing I needed was a bunny feasting on them for lunch.

"Hey!" I snapped at the animal. "Get away from my vines!"

The rabbit froze, trembled, and then sped off across the field. It disappeared into a hole, down into its burrow.

I immediately felt ashamed for scaring such a defenseless creature. It's not like it had many other options for food out here among all these dead crops. I would leave some strawberries outside for it later.

Before I went inside, I placed a series of wooden stakes in the ground in the path of the vines. One of my guidebooks had said that the tendrils would wrap around anything in their path, as if they had a mind of their own. They could even crawl up a fence, defying gravity.

That night at dinner, I was in such a good mood that I didn't groan when my parents discussed which cheesy pun to print on the labels for Dunn Farms Jams. I even volunteered to go out with a sponge and a bucket to scrub the paint off our sign, until it no longer spelled "Doom."

I was nervous at school the next day. What if Charlie had another prank in store for me?

Fortunately, I made it through the entire day without a Charlie sighting. His pumpkin pulp trick must have backfired enough that he had decided to leave me alone—at least for now. When school was over, I invited my new friend Yvonne back to the house to show her the pumpkin patch.

The vines had grown at an incredible rate over the last twenty-four hours. They had snaked through the dirt, wrapping around the sticks I had left, just as the gardening books said they would.

The plants also seemed to be reaching out to each other. They had formed lines between the mounds I had dug, making the triangle look even more like some weird alien symbol.

"Wow!" Yvonne said. She bent down to touch one of the shimmering blue flowers that had blossomed overnight. "Pumpkins are so funny looking. I never expected them to come from such a beautiful plant."

"The flowers are supposed to be orange, but this is a special variety," I explained. I pointed to one of the blossoms, where a lump the size of a golf ball was already growing beneath the petals. "The pumpkins themselves grow after the flowers have been pollinated. When the pumpkin gets big enough, the flowers fall away."

I was about to explain more when I heard an odd sound. Something was whimpering near us. When I listened more closely, I realized the noise was coming from the pumpkin patch itself.

"Do you hear that?" I asked Yvonne. She nodded. The pumpkin leaves were so thick it was hard to see the ground beneath. I followed the noise to the largest plant, in the center of the triangle.

When I pulled aside a dense group of leaves, my breath caught in my throat.

The rabbit that had been nibbling on my plants yesterday had returned.

That had been a deadly mistake.

Because today, the pumpkin vines had coiled completely around its white, furry body.

It continued to whimper and try to wriggle free, but the tendrils held it tight, flattening its floppy ears to its back. The end of the vine had even begun to wrap around the poor creature's throat. I wondered how long it had been trapped here.

I got down on my knees and carefully untangled the vine. The rabbit quivered beneath my hands as I freed it.

Finally, I untied the last coil, which had looped around one of the creature's hind legs. The rabbit gave an angry hiss at the plant. Then it scampered off, sprinting as fast and far away as it could.

If I had known what the next few weeks would bring, I would have run, too.

13

On the third day, the first pumpkins began to grow. There were four of them, one for each vine. I should have been overjoyed, but I immediately knew something was wrong.

These pumpkins were all blue.

At first, I thought that maybe they would ripen into a normal shade of orange. After all, my guidebook told me that they usually started out green until the sun warmed them over time.

Instead, as the pumpkins grew larger each day, the blue became more vivid, the color of tropical ocean waters.

Soon they were as tall as my waist. Dark purple veins spread through their bumpy rinds like spider webs.

What could I have done wrong? I had been following Abel's instructions exactly the way he had written. I watered and fertilized them every day.

I imagined bringing blue pumpkins to the Jack-o'-lantern Festival. Charlie would mock me for sure if I showed up with these. "The city girl is so dumb she doesn't even know what color a pumpkin is supposed to be!" he would say between laughs.

That Saturday, I pedaled my bike through town and down the narrow lane to Abel's seed shop. Maybe the gardener would know what to do with his creations to make them look normal.

An older woman with gray hair was sweeping the shop's porch. She peered at me through her bifocals as I pulled up on my bike. "Well, I'll be!" she said. A friendly smile spread across her face. "You must be little Jimmy Dunn's daughter."

"How did you know?" I asked, taken aback. I glanced at her name tag, which read "ANNABELLE" in capital letters.

"I was one of your father's teachers way back when he was your age, before I retired to tend this shop full-time," she explained. "I'd heard he moved back to town with his daughter, and I'd recognize that nose of his anywhere."

I touched my nose self-consciously. "I hope that's a good thing."

The woman leaned her broom against the wall and gestured for me to follow her into the shop. "What can I do for you today, puddin'? Some petunia seeds? Maybe some spicy chili peppers if you're feeling brave?"

I shook my head. "I got some pumpkin seeds here last Sunday, and I just had some questions about how to properly care for them. They're turning out a little bit … strange."

Annabelle stopped in her tracks. She squinted at me in confusion. "Are you sure you're at the right shop? I never open for business on Sundays, and I definitely would have remembered you coming to visit. It's a small town."

I shook my head. "No, it must have been your son running the shop that day. Abel was very nice, and he gave me the seeds for free—"

"I don't have a son," Annabelle interrupted me. "And since my husband passed away last year, I've been the only person who runs this store. I can't afford to hire any help."

An unsettling feeling knotted my stomach. Something wasn't right. Now that I was paying more attention, even the shop looked different than it had just a week ago. The weird glass specimen jars had disappeared from the shelves.

Annabelle was starting to look concerned. "Honey, are you feeling okay? Your face is white as a ghost. Why don't you sit down and I'll get you a cup of tea from the pot I just boiled."

I didn't want to sit down. I had just noticed something odd on Annabelle's name tag. There was a sticky residue on either side of her name.

It looked like there had been tape on it recently to cover some of the letters.

And when you crossed off the beginning and end of "ANNABELLE" ...

... You were left with "ABEL."

The room spun around me. If Abel wasn't a shopkeeper, who was the man I had met with the previous week?

Then I had an even more terrifying thought:

What if he was still here?

I needed to know. I staggered through the rows of shelves, heading for the back of the shop. I heard Annabelle distantly call my name.

When I reached the back door, I took a deep breath and threw it open, expecting to find the stranger lurking in the greenhouse of bizarre plants.

Instead, I found myself staring at an empty back-yard with a few lemon trees growing in it. A light breeze whisked around me.

Just like the man who had called himself Abel, the greenhouse had vanished off the face of the earth.

II

THE DAY OF THE JACK-O'-LANTERN FESTIVAL

14

M y parents stood to either side of me next to the pumpkin patch.

My mom whistled. "I can't believe it," she said. "These are officially the biggest pumpkins I have ever seen."

She wasn't kidding. Over the last few weeks, the pumpkins had all grown monstrously large. Three of them had nearly reached my height.

The fourth pumpkin in the center of the patch had grown faster than the others. When it rained, it would absorb the water right out of the soil, leaving the patch completely dry almost as soon as the raindrops landed. It must have sucked up all the nutrients too, because the grass in the surrounding area had withered and died.

Now the pumpkin was twice my height and heavier than a car. It looked like a gigantic blue meteorite had fallen from the sky.

My father beamed with pride. "It's finally happening. After forty years, I'm finally going to beat Zeke Slade at the pumpkin competition."

My mother cleared her throat and glared at him.

Dad grinned sheepishly. "I mean, *Kayla* is going to beat him. What matters is that the Dunn family name will finally get engraved on that trophy."

"I'm really proud of you," Mom said. She ruffled my hair. "I know moving away from your friends must have been hard, but you really poured your heart and soul into this pumpkin patch. When I start growing my own fruits for Dunn Farms Jams, you're going to have to give *me* some gardening pointers!"

I couldn't help but smile, too. The memory of Abel and the vanishing greenhouse seemed like a distant dream at this point. In a way, he had been my guardian angel.

"One thing is for sure," I said. "Dunn Farms Jams might have to branch out into pies, because we are going to have *a lot* of pumpkin to eat."

"I have just the recipe for the occasion!" Mom replied.

Something honked behind us. A forklift drove

around the corner of the house. My father's friend waved from behind the wheel. The largest pumpkin was so massive that we needed heavy machinery to transport it to the Jack-o'-Lantern Festival.

While Dad and his friend began to load the gigantic pumpkin, I drove into town with Mom. I had agreed to help her set up our farm's booth for the first day of the festival. She had been slaving over vats of boiling jam for the last two weeks to prepare for her "grand opening," so I figured the least I could do was help.

The Festival was even bigger than I had imagined. The town hosted it each year in the sprawling apple orchard and the celebration lasted an entire weekend. Farmers and craftsmen came from miles around to decorate their booths, which formed a small city under the apple trees. As we walked through the fair, I watched carpenters setting up a large stage and rows of chairs. My pumpkin would be weighed in this theater tomorrow, along with all its competitors. It was hard to imagine Charlie having a pumpkin bigger than the monster my dad was currently driving here with the forklift.

By the time we finished setting up the booth, we had stacked a wall of jam jars so high that I had to stand on my tiptoes to peer over it. A few early customers approached the booth to chat with my mom and spread samples on the homemade biscuits we had baked. As the crowd grew, Mom gave me her blessing to wander off and explore the fair.

I found Yvonne helping her father ladle out his cinnamon apple cider into sample cups. As soon as she spotted me, she dropped the spoon back into the steel vat. "Come on!" she said excitedly, grabbing my hand and dragging me away. "If this is your first time at the festival, you have to see the Cannonball."

"Cannonball?" I echoed as she tugged me through the maze of booths. "Where are you taking me, a pirate ship?"

Yvonne smirked at me. "You have so much to learn, new girl."

Eventually the booths thinned out and we reached the river that snaked through the orchard. We followed it until we arrived at the waterfall. Since my last visit, someone had anchored a wooden platform out in the rapids. It floated just a few lengths before the water disappeared over the edge.

I gulped as Yvonne jumped fearlessly onto the raft. I was still terrified of the waterfall, but I couldn't let my new friend think I was a total wuss.

I tried to keep my expression calm as I took a nervous step onto the platform. It rocked beneath me and I grabbed the railing so hard that my knuckles turned white.

In the middle of the raft was an enormous pumpkin. It wasn't quite as large as the one I had grown, but it was still as tall as I was, and at least it was the proper color.

"Touch it," Yvonne instructed me.

I looked at her in confusion. Then I cautiously placed my hands against the pumpkin. The moment my skin made contact with the orange rind, I shivered and pulled away.

It was ice cold to the touch.

"After each festival, the town takes the winning pumpkin and stores it in a freezer for an entire year," Yvonne explained. She pointed to the puddle forming beneath it. "Then they defrost it at the next year's festival, carve it into a gigantic jack-o'-lantern, and light a big fire inside of it."

"Why do they call it the Cannonball, though?" I asked.

"Good question!" Yvonne led me over to the edge of the platform. Someone had built a wide chute, like a water slide—only if you slid down it, you would be swept right over the falls. I shuddered.

Yvonne touched a wooden lever. "For the festival's finale, everyone gathers in the valley below. Up here, they load the burning jack-o'-lantern into the chute. After the crowd counts down from ten to zero, the mayor pulls this lever. The lever lowers the chute's safety bar, and the jack-o'-lantern tumbles into the water—then floats right over the falls." With her hands, she mimicked the pumpkin falling and then a *splat* motion. "The moment the burning pumpkin hits the pool below, a massive splash soaks the crowd and everyone yells 'Cannonball!'"

That did sound awesome. I also felt like I would appreciate the waterfall a lot more if I was standing safely at the bottom, instead of the top.

When I turned back to Yvonne, I noticed that she was staring over my shoulder. Her eyes had gone wide and she was trembling.

"What's the matter?" I asked her.

I spun around—

—and came face to face with a tall masked man wielding a chainsaw.

15

I opened my mouth to scream but only a hoarse wheeze came out. The figure lumbered forward one step, two steps. His apron was splattered with a dark orange substance. His menacing eyes peered out from the slits in a plastic mask. The saw blade gleamed in his hands.

Then he reached up with his free hand and ripped off his mask.

The tall gangly man had floppy red hair that matched the constellation of freckles across his cheeks. He grinned a blindingly white smile at the two of us. Without his mask, he looked far less sinister. "Hello!" he greeted us with a big wave in a warm, booming voice. "I knew a crowd would gather to watch me carve the Cannonball! I just thought there would be more of you."

Now it all made sense. I glanced between the chainsaw and the giant pumpkin. Of course, you would need more than a puny knife to carve one of that size.

While I gawked silently, still at a loss for words, Yvonne cleared her throat. "Of course, Mr. Slade," she said, pretending as though this man hadn't just scared us half to death. "I wouldn't miss the carving for the world!"

"Mr. Slade?" I repeated. "As in Ezekiel Slade?" Could this jolly giant somehow be the same nemesis that tormented my father as a kid? And also be the father of *my* tormentor? The longer I stared at him, the more his resemblance to Charlie became obvious.

Their personalities could not have been more different, though.

"You've heard of me? I didn't know I was so famous in these here parts!" Mr. Slade threw back his head and laughed from deep in his belly. When he was done, he stuck out his hand for me to shake. "My friends call me Zeke, and *you* are a friend. Pleased to make your acquaintance."

"Kayla Dunn," I said as his hand enveloped mine. "I think you grew up with my father."

Zeke held me out at arm's length and studied my face. "Well I'll be darned—I'd heard Jimmy was back in town." He gave me a troubled frown, an expression I bet this happy-go-lucky man rarely used. "I'm ashamed to admit that I wasn't the nicest person to your dad back in the day, but I hope he's forgiven me. I suppose I was always envious of him."

"It was a long time ago. I'm sure he doesn't even remember," I lied.

Zeke's contagious grin returned. "Tell Jimmy you're all invited over for a big dinner at Slade Farms next week, to formally welcome him back to the neighborhood. Have you met my boy Charlie yet?"

I glanced sidelong at Yvonne, who wrinkled her nose. "Once or twice," I said emotionlessly.

"Yvonne, you and your dad should join, too," Zeke added. "Charlie will be elated to have company."

As nice as Zeke was, I was concerned by how little he seemed to know his son.

Still, Yvonne and I both graciously accepted his invite. For the next half hour, we watched as Zeke revved up the chainsaw and cut the top off the thawing pumpkin. Even from a safe distance, we occasionally got hit with a splash of gooey pulp. It took a stepladder, a shovel, and a wheelbarrow for Zeke to hollow out the inside.

The best part was when he handed markers to Yvonne and me. "As the future of Orchard Falls, I think you two should do the honors of drawing this jack-o'-lantern the scariest face you can," Zeke said. "I'm sure you're both better artists than I am. I can barely draw a stick figure, and I *am* one!" He followed up his joke with another massive belly laugh that echoed into the valley below.

Yvonne drew eyes and a pair of horns while I outlined several rows of jagged fangs. After we finished, Zeke carved out our creation. For the final touch, he filled the hollow interior with a cluster of torches.

We all stood back and admired our handiwork. The flames crackled in the jack-o'-lantern's demonic eyes and grin.

Yvonne clapped her hands together. "It's beautiful," she proclaimed. "In, like, a creepy sort of way."

"Yeah," I agreed. "Almost a shame that it's going to explode into a million pieces tomorrow."

"Almost!" Zeke threw back his head and laughed one last time.

My stomach growled as I made my way back to the Dunn Farms Jams booth. I had been so distracted decorating the Cannonball that I had forgotten to eat lunch. Fortunately, the first day of the festival concluded with a community potluck dinner in the town hall. People brought dishes of all kinds to share in a massive buffet.

As I helped Mom pack up her remaining jam jars, she suddenly straightened up in a panic and groaned. "Oh, blast! I forgot the peach tarts I made for the potluck at home. I'll have to go back and get them."

I noticed how exhausted she looked. "Let me walk home to get them," I volunteered. "I can put them in the basket on my bike and race back here in no time." When she opened her mouth to protest, I added, "Come on, I could use an excuse to change my clothes." I pointed to the pumpkin pulp splattered across my overalls.

Relief washed across my mother's face. "Just try to get back into town before dark," she said. "They hired a bluegrass band to play at dinner. I'd hate for you to miss any of the show!"

The sun was already beginning to set by the time I jogged the mile back to Dunn Farms. The sweet aroma of my mother's peach tarts lingered in the kitchen. I felt my stomach rumble again with hunger. "I'll feed you soon," I promised my gut.

As I pulled the foil-wrapped trays of tarts out of

the fridge, I glanced out the window. The rays of the dusk sun illuminated the field in an electric shade of orange. When my eyes fell on my pumpkins, I immediately could tell something was wrong.

I raced out the back door and over to the patch. My father had already transported the largest pumpkin away—that much didn't bother me. However, where the three smaller gourds should have been intact, only two remained.

The third pumpkin had been destroyed.

16

The pumpkin rind lay in two halves. It was as if someone had taken a gigantic axe and cleaved it right down the middle. A blue smear of pulp trailed off into the cornfield like an ugly brushstroke.

"No, no, no!" I cried, dropping to my knees beside the decimated pumpkin. What could possibly have happened?

Had Dad and his friend accidentally run over it with the forklift? He promised me they would be careful while they were loading the larger one.

The pumpkin had been so big that an animal couldn't have done this. No, someone had to have deliberately caused this sort of destruction.

There was only one person I could think of with

the motive to sabotage my weeks of hard work like this.

I gave a low, furious growl and rolled up my flannel sleeves as I followed the trail of pulp into the field. Cornstalks had been flattened along the way. Charlie must have dragged away a piece of the rind as a trophy after he destroyed it.

Well, if I could trace this trail back to Slade Farms, I would have all the evidence I needed to pin the vandalism on him. We would see who was laughing when the police showed up at his doorstep.

The pulp trail eventually took a sharp turn in the cornfield. I emerged next to a small pond on the outskirts of our property.

The blue path seemed to end behind a large boulder on the water's edge.

I crept closer, moving as stealthily as I could through the mud. On the other side of the boulder, I heard a splashing sound.

The culprit was still here. Had Charlie really been brazen enough to hang around the scene of the crime and go for a dip in our pond? The *nerve* of him.

Well, the scare-master was about to get a scare of his own. I inched closer to the boulder. I drew in a deep breath.

Then I jumped around the stone and let loose a

banshee scream that would haunt Charlie's nightmares for years to come.

Only it wasn't Charlie who was waiting for me on the other side.

I quickly cut my scream short. It transformed into a terrified gurgle in the back of my throat.

A creature hunched over the pond's edge, lapping up water. Its sleek blue exoskeleton fluoresced softly in the dying light of the evening.

It must have been six feet long, with more legs than I could count and two gigantic claws with razor-sharp pincers. An armor-plated tail curved into a crescent above it. The tail ended in a stinger the size of a butcher's knife that glistened with venom.

When the creature heard my scream, it slowly rotated to face me. The joints of its spindly legs clicked away as it moved.

I stood frozen in place watching it, too afraid to make any sudden movements. Thorns and vines crisscrossed its exoskeleton. They throbbed to the beat of its heart, like pulsing veins. The leafy tendrils curled and reached out for me with a mind of their own. One of them brushed my cheek.

The creature was half-scorpion.

Half-plant.

100% nightmare.

And it had hatched from one of the pumpkins I had grown.

No, not pumpkins, I realized.

All this time, I had been growing *eggs*.

Maybe the scorpion was like the dinosaurs I had seen in movies, with vision based on movement. Maybe if I continued to stand still, it would never even know I was there.

All that hope evaporated as its four glowing eyes focused on me.

It bared its fangs and hissed.

Then its stinger came plunging down, aimed straight for my heart.

17

I dove to the side just as the creature's stinger sliced through the space where I had been standing. The tip struck the boulder with such incredible force that stone exploded in a cloud of dust. The mammoth scorpion howled in pain.

I scampered backward as its stinger stabbed down again and again. Mud splashed over me every time the barb missed and plunged into the earth.

I somehow regained my balance and took off sprinting. I heard the rapid-fire *snap-snap-snap* of its pincers nipping at my heels.

As I bolted away from the pond, I risked a glance over my shoulder. The monster's legs had gotten stuck in the mud, but not for long. With a frustrated squawk, it propelled itself free and resumed pursuit.

My feet pounded over the grassy field. For a moment, I thought that maybe, just maybe, I had a chance of outrunning the creature. Maybe my two legs could move more quickly than its eight. Maybe I could retreat to the safety of the farmhouse and slam the door before it caught up to me. I would call the local sheriff, and the county police force would show up to stop this monstrosity.

Then I tripped.

My foot snagged on something hidden in the grass. I landed hard next to an old stone water well.

Meanwhile, the scorpion closed the distance between us. It raced across the tall grass, eager to make me its first meal.

I was about to start running again when I realized the object I had tripped over was a rope. One end was attached to the well. The other end was tied to a wooden bucket.

Suddenly, I had a crazy idea. It might save my life —or it might just get me killed.

The scorpion slowed down, sensing victory over its prey. I trembled as the disgusting creature approached. Its raw, pungent stink was overwhelming. I forced myself to remain still as its lethal stinger curved upward, ready to strike.

The venomous tip darted forward like a lightning

bolt, but I was prepared. I thrust the bucket into its path.

The stinger's barb punctured the bucket and emerged out the other side. It stopped just a few inches from my face. I could see my warped, terrified reflection in the shiny surface of the stinger. I quickly let go of the bucket and started running again.

The creature attempted to pursue me, but it didn't make it far. When it was just within reach, its body abruptly jerked to a halt.

It tried to come at me again, but to no avail. The newborn monster screeched, confused why it had stopped moving.

Its stinger was lodged in the bucket. The thick rope attached to it had tethered the creature to the well.

I had put the scorpion on a leash.

I offered a silent thank-you to the farmer who had built that well, but I knew my trap wouldn't last long. Even now, the wooden frame groaned as the scorpion viciously tugged against it. I needed to get help before it broke free.

18

As I raced into the cornfield, back toward the farm, I had another horrifying thought: if my pumpkins really were some sort of monster eggs, then the scorpion I had just bested was only the beginning. There were still two more back at the farm.

The largest one of all was currently in the middle of the country fair …

… Only a short distance from the town hall where my parents and everyone in Orchard Falls were sitting down to eat dinner.

My luck only got worse as I emerged from the cornfield. It didn't look like the two remaining eggs had hatched yet—thank goodness.

However, I found a different unwelcome visitor waiting for me in my pumpkin patch.

Charlie had a knife in his hand. With angry strokes, he carved letters into one of the pumpkins. Pulp oozed through the slashes.

Charlie had just started to form the "R" in "LOSER" when he noticed me running out of the cornfield. At first, he stiffened, looking guilty that I had caught him in the act. He had probably expected me to be at the potluck supper with the rest of the town. I would come home to the cruel message carved into my pumpkin, while he laughed from the safety of the shadows.

I was so out of breath from running that it was hard to get words out. "Charlie," I wheezed. "You need … to get out of here … now."

His expression changed from alarmed to defiant. "I'm not going anywhere, new girl," he snarled.

I glanced back in the direction of the old well. "You don't understand—"

"No, *you* don't understand," Charlie interrupted. He poked my mud-stained overalls. "This is *my* town. The Jack-o'-Lantern Festival is the one thing I look forward to year after year. Standing on that stage and accepting the first-place ribbon for *my* pumpkin. The whole town cheering as it becomes the next festival's Cannonball. Then one day you come waltzing into Orchard Falls with your weird blue pumpkins and think you can take all that away from me." He jabbed a finger at me again. "Who exactly do you think you are?"

He was not picking up on my sense of urgency. "Look," I started to say, "the pumpkins don't matter right now——"

"See, that's exactly why you don't deserve to win!" he cried. "*The pumpkins don't matter?* You don't really care about them. If you knew even the first thing about pumpkins, yours might have come out the right color!" He knocked hard on the egg behind him.

"Charlie," I tried to warn him.

But he kept on ranting and raving about how I was an unwelcome intruder and had no place here in Orchard Falls.

If he hadn't been facing me, he would have seen the egg behind him start to quiver.

He would have heard the first few cracks in the shell as the creature within stirred.

And he definitely would have seen the glowing eye appear in the "O" he had carved.

"Charlie!" I screamed this time, finally getting him to pause. I pointed a shaking finger behind him. "Monster!"

He must have thought I was pointing at him because he hollered back, "I am *not* a monster!"

That was the moment that the egg behind him exploded.

19

The egg's shell burst into a thousand pieces. A wave of the stinking slime washed over Charlie, instantly painting him blue. He wiped the ooze from his hair and examined his fingers in confusion.

The creature behind him emerged from the egg's remains. It slowly uncurled itself from a fetal ball. Mucus dripped off its exoskeleton. Its joints cracked as it stretched its long legs for the first time.

Charlie slowly turned to look at the gigantic scorpion. A low whimper escaped his mouth.

I started to back away, but Charlie had frozen, too petrified to move.

The scorpion wobbled on its feet at first. Maybe it was like a human child—maybe it needed time to learn how to walk.

Something told me it would be a fast learner.

I rushed forward, seized Charlie by the elbow, and screamed, "Run!"

My voice startled him back into action. The creature stood between the farmhouse and us, so I pointed to our next best hope for shelter:

The barn.

Side by side, we sprinted for the wooden structure. When I dared to glance back, the creature fixed its glowing eyes on me and began to skitter in our direction.

Charlie and I passed through the barn's entrance and immediately worked together to push the heavy doors closed. I lowered the thick bolt to lock them together.

It wasn't a moment too soon. The scorpion struck the wood from the outside like a battering ram. The doors buckled inward but the latch held—for now.

"What on earth did you plant?" Charlie shouted at me, panting. "I *knew* your stupid pumpkins were too big to be true."

"Don't worry, we'll have plenty of time for you to lecture me about what a cheater I am—when we're digesting in that thing's stomach!" I snapped. "Now do you want to live or not?"

Charlie swallowed and nodded.

While the creature's claws pounded against the doors, I led Charlie over to the ladder and climbed up to the loft. If we couldn't outrun the scorpion, then maybe we could at least hide from it.

Once I reached the top, I steadied the rickety ladder as Charlie climbed up after me. The pounding on the doors had stopped. "Looks like that stupid critter gave up," Charlie said, sounding hopeful.

Then through the silence, I heard the whisper of something speeding over the dried cornstalks outside.

The monster hit the doors so hard that they snapped right off their hinges. Splinters showered the inside of the barn like confetti. The mangled doors slammed to the ground.

The scorpion stood triumphantly in the entrance where they used to be.

Charlie was so surprised that his sweaty hands slipped off the top rung of the ladder. I reached out to grab him, but missed.

He fell ten feet to the barn floor, flailing the whole way down.

20

"Charlie!" I cried out. He groaned and tried to pick himself up off the floor, then collapsed back to the hay. The fall must have rattled him bad.

The creature skittered closer to him. Its pincers snapped hungrily, preparing to dissect their dinner.

I frantically searched around for something I could use to attack it. The loft was empty except for mounds of moldy straw.

Then my gaze fell on the large hay bale dangling from the ceiling.

A few weeks ago, when I had walked through the barn with my father, he had pointed up at the bale. "Be careful around that," he had warned me. "I know hay seems light when you pick up one straw of it, but compacted like that, the bale probably weighs a thousand pounds."

"Then how do they get it up there?" I had asked.

He had shown me how the chain was threaded through a pulley in the rafters. The other end of the chain was secured in place by a winch, a device that let you raise or lower the bale by turning a crank.

As the creature closed in on Charlie, I followed the bale's chain with my eyes, until I found the winch. It was attached to one of the loft's support beams.

I waited in anticipation until the creature crossed beneath the shadow of the bale.

Then I released the brake that held the crank in place.

The bale dropped a few inches, but suddenly stopped. I looked upward in frustration. The chain had snagged on the rusted pulley.

I only had one more shot at this. The monster would be on Charlie in a matter of moments.

I took off running across the loft. With a war cry, I pounced onto the dangling hay bale.

The impact of my body did the trick. The rusted pulley above snapped free from the rafters. My stomach lurched as if I were on a roller coaster as the block of hay beneath me dropped.

The creature only had a second to squeal as the

bale came crashing down on him, flattening him to the floor.

I climbed down off the mound of hay and gazed upon the aftermath. The creature had disappeared entirely beneath the bale, except for a single claw. For a moment, I watched the pincers open and reach out for me, and I worried that maybe my plan had failed.

Then the claw stiffened before going limp altogether. It dropped to the floorboards with a heavy thud.

I breathed a sigh of relief and helped Charlie back to his feet. He still looked dazed, but managed a pained smile. "That was a pretty impressive leap, Kayla Dunn," he said. "You should think about trying out for the basketball team."

A low growl interrupted our celebration. We turned to find another scorpion standing in the broken entryway. At first, I thought the third egg had hatched. Then I noticed the bucket still stuck to the creature's tail. The first one had finally escaped my trap.

And it looked angrier than ever.

21

As the scorpion advanced, Charlie and I slowly backed away, toward the rear of the barn. "Why does this one have a bucket on its tail?" Charlie stammered.

I grabbed a rusty shovel off the wall, the only weapon I could find. "Because I tied it to the old well," I replied.

Charlie pointed at the frayed end of the rope trailing behind the creature. "That thing has gigantic scissors for hands, and you thought you could tie it up with *string*?"

"Well, I'm sorry," I snapped. "The monster-hunting store was fresh out of giant scorpion traps."

The creature skittered over the mound of hay that had crushed the other one. It poked at its sibling's unmoving claw. When it got no response, it let loose a bloodcurdling howl. Its eyes gleamed with vengeance as they focused on me.

Then it lunged.

Charlie and I dove in opposite directions as the scorpion sailed through the hair. It collided with the back wall so hard I thought the barn would implode. Dust rained down from the rafters.

With the two of us on either side of it, the creature had to make a decision. Unfortunately for Charlie, he was the closest. When he tried to dart for the exit, the scorpion swept its tail along the floor, tripping him to the ground. Charlie fell hard for the second time in the last five minutes. I watched the sleek blue tail extend back, ready to skewer him.

I glanced at the barn doors. If there was a time to run, this was my only shot.

But I knew I had to intervene.

I raised the shovel in my hands over my head and brought it down hard like a hammer on the creature's back. I targeted a spot where the exoskeleton was exposed between the vines.

Clang. The impact reverberated through my arms. To my alarm, the shovel barely dented the scorpion's armor plating.

The monster turned to me. I jabbed at it with the

shovel, trying to keep it out of claw's reach. I heard Charlie's footsteps treading across the barn floor as he rushed for the doors. *Coward*, I thought.

As I thrust the shovel at the scorpion, aiming for its face with all of my might, one of its claws shot forward. The pincers clamped down on the shovel's wooden shaft. With an effortless squeeze, it sliced my weapon in two. The metal top clattered hopelessly to the floor, leaving me with only a broken stake.

A low moan escaped my throat as I realized that the creature had me cornered. This was it. My last thought was a prayer that Charlie made it to town to warn the others so my parents could get safely away.

S uddenly the dark barn filled with light. I heard a
deep rumble, and briefly wondered if lightning
had struck the field outside. Then the light grew
brighter, so intense that I threw up my hands to block
it out.

The creature, too, turned to search for the source
of the light.

It released a panicked squawk as the old tractor
blindsided it. The headlights illuminated its surprised
eyes for one fleeting moment before it was crushed
between the tractor's front grill and one of the barn's
support beams. The exoskeleton gave a resounding
crack and exploded in a mess of blue goo.

A shaken but triumphant Charlie stepped down

from behind the wheel of the tractor. He held out a hand to pull to my feet.

"You saved my life," I said.

He smirked. "Couldn't let you be the only hero in Orchard Falls."

"It's always a competition with you," I muttered.

Smoke rose from the tractor's engine, which was stuck in the creature's carcass. It gave a final whine of protest before it died altogether. "Looks like we're biking into town," I said. Then I had a chilling realization. I grabbed Charlie's wrist. "Charlie—there's still another egg out there."

We rushed outside and over to the pumpkin patch. To our relief, the final of the three small eggs had yet to hatch. "Must be a late bloomer," Charlie said.

As soon as he said that, the egg quivered, as though the thing inside had heard him. Our eyes widened in unison.

I pointed to the metal silo, which gleamed under the light of the full moon. "We have to get it in there before it hatches!"

Charlie looked skeptical, and for a moment, I thought he was going to take off toward town. Finally, he nodded and joined me behind the giant egg.

Together we began to push. The egg was roundest in the middle, so we would be able to roll it like a wheel if we could tip it over.

It was even heavier than I thought, more than both our weights combined. We dug our heels into the soil and grunted, pressing our shoulders into the rind. The field sloped downhill between the patch and the silo. If we could just get some momentum ...

We both doubled our efforts and finally the egg tipped up, up, until with a thud, it landed on its round edge.

A growl of discontent echoed from somewhere inside.

If the creature hadn't been ready to emerge yet before, it definitely was now.

"We don't have much time!" I shouted to Charlie as we started to roll it toward the silo. My arms burned from the effort. I could see my companion sweating, but it got a little easier as the egg picked up speed.

We were halfway down the hill when a claw erupted from the shell.

23

The pincers burst through the rind where the stem used to be. The claw thrashed about, trying to clamp down on the two of us for daring to disturb its slumber. I jumped just in time as it snapped at my ankles, slicing through a tuft of dried grass like a lawnmower.

Charlie and I pushed it the last twenty feet to the silo, while chunks of the egg fell away piece by piece. With a final heave, we shoved it hard through the open gate.

Momentum carried the egg across the silo floor. When it smashed into the metal wall in back, the shell split in two. A slimy newborn scorpion spilled out onto the floor. It spotted us immediately and scampered toward the open entrance.

Charlie and I slammed the sliding door closed just as the creature plowed into it. We jumped back as its pincers punched the steel, making tiny dents. The door was too thick and strong for it.

Hopefully, this scorpion wouldn't be getting free anytime soon.

"We can figure out what to do with this one later," I told Charlie between deep breaths. As much as I wanted to collapse to the dirt and catch my breath, there was no time.

The largest egg waited for us at the Jack-o'-Lantern Festival.

For all we knew, it could have hatched already. As we spoke, the beast within might be terrorizing the unsuspecting residents of Orchard Falls as they sat down for their potluck supper. I pictured my parents huddled in the corner of the town hall as the scorpion tore off the roof, saliva dripping from its jaws as it loomed over them …

I only hoped that we weren't too late.

24

We made it back to the festival in record time. Charlie was faster than I was, and I had to push myself to the limit to keep up.

Night had fully descended by the time we reached the fair, and so had a thick mist. The fog blanketed the orchard so densely that it was hard to see more than twenty feet in front of us.

Fortunately, the town had lined the pathways between the booths with hundreds of lit jack-o'-lanterns. The firelight tinted the mist with an eerie orange glow.

Even creepier: the festival was completely deserted. Not a single soul remained behind in the booths.

We abandoned our bikes outside the fair's main

stage. The open-air theater was dark as we entered, except for what little moonlight filtered through the mist.

"The spotlight is around here somewhere," Charlie whispered. I heard him stumbling around in the darkness for a few moments, then the sound of a metal switch flipping. We both winced as light flooded the stage.

When my eyes adjusted, I let myself relax a little. The massive egg was still intact. It dwarfed the other pumpkins. If it had actually participated in tomorrow's competition, it probably would have broken the scale when they weighed it.

"What are we even going to do with this thing?" Charlie asked as we passed down the center aisle between rows of folding chairs.

"I hadn't thought that far ahead," I admitted. Hay bales and tractors might have defeated the others, but if the size of the egg indicated the size of the creature, it was probably big enough to *eat* any tractor we drove at it.

I climbed onto the stage and hesitantly approached the egg. I couldn't hear any sounds coming from within, but when I dared to touch the shell, I felt it gently pulsating.

Like a heartbeat.

Out in the amphitheater, someone started to clap.

I shielded my eyes from the spotlight and squinted as I searched for the source of the applause. The seats had all been empty when we entered. Now a tall man occupied a spot in the front row, as though he had materialized out of thin air.

The man who had given me the seeds—the one who had called himself Abel—grinned up at me.

25

Abel had replaced his farmer's overalls with a white lab coat and pair of amber goggles that concealed his eyes. "Bravo," he said, still applauding. "I knew you had a fire burning in you, Kayla, but I never expected these eggs to turn out *so* beautifully."

I froze. Somehow, this man now seemed far more terrifying than the giant scorpions. "What do you want, Abel?" I asked. "Or whoever you really are."

He rose from his chair, drawing himself up to his full towering height. "My name," he said slowly, "is Dr. Umbra. And I just came to thank you for doing my handiwork for me." His face glowed with pride as he gazed up at the gigantic egg, like a father holding his newborn for the first time.

Charlie moved beside me. "Kayla, who is this

99

creep?" he whispered. His body had gone rigid, as though he were expecting a fight. He could sense this man was dangerous.

"I'm not a creep, Charles," Dr. Umbra corrected him. "I'm a *visionary*."

Every time he took a step closer to the stage, I backed up. This man's not-so-little pets had nearly killed me not once but four times tonight. "Why me?" I asked. "Why not grow these freaks yourself, in your twisted little greenhouse?"

"Because I'm a busy man," Dr. Umbra replied. "The *scorpikins* are just one of many projects that require my attention. So as an experiment I thought: what if I could just get others to grow my children for me? But first, I needed a test run—you—to make sure that my babies would grow here."

Something about the way he said the last word unsettled me. "What do you mean by *here*? Orchard Falls?"

Dr. Umbra reached up and pulled off his googles, revealing his eyes. They glowed tangerine like two simmering coals. What he said next chilled me to the bone:

"Here on Earth."

26

I shuddered. *Here on Earth?*

The day we had met, Dr. Umbra hadn't been kidding when he said he wasn't from around here.

Charlie took a brave step forward, even though I'm not sure he understood what was going on quite yet. "Well, you've failed," he said. "We've already defeated the others. This egg is next."

Dr. Umbra sighed deeply. "It is a real pity that you murdered my drones before they even had a chance to grow to their full potential."

I exchanged a look with Charlie. Those scorpions were supposed to get *even bigger*?

"No matter," the doctor continued. "All that truly matters now is the queen."

On cue, the egg next to us quivered.

Dr. Umbra drew a silver object from his lab coat pocket—a bell the size of an apple. "She seems reluctant to hatch. Perhaps she's experiencing a little stage fright. Let's speed up the process and encourage her to make her grand debut, shall we?"

With a swing of his hand, he rang the bell. A crisp note sounded through the amphitheater. When it chimed again, I felt it reverberate deep in my bones.

A low rumble echoed through the hall. It took me a moment to realize the sound was coming from inside the egg.

It was not a happy noise.

The third time Dr. Umbra rang the bell, a crack ruptured through the shell. Charlie and I instinctively jumped back. The line zigzagged through the veiny rind, from top to bottom.

On the fourth chime, the top half of the egg erupted like a volcano. A tidal wave of goo gushed over us, soaking our clothes and nearly washing us right off the stage. The stench was unimaginable.

What remained of the egg split open in two halves.

The creature that emerged made the smaller ones look like they belonged in a petting zoo.

Thorns longer than my arms formed spiky rows

across the queen's hulking exoskeleton. Her claws looked large and sharp enough to shear through a tree trunk in a single snip. A vine-like tongue darted out of her open jaws, flicking pungent drool at us.

Dr. Umbra gazed up at his creation. Tears of joy welled in his eyes. "You are so much more beautiful than I ever could have dreamed," he whispered.

Charlie and I snapped out of the hypnotic spell of the hatching and jumped off the stage. As we dashed down the center aisle, Dr. Umbra didn't try to stop us. He just gave the bell one final ring. The scorpion queen tilted her head back and let loose a nightmarish wail.

It was the kind of noise that made me feel like I would never be safe again.

"Do you hear that?" Dr. Umbra called after us. "That is the sound of your doom."

Charlie and I sprinted out into the orchard and climbed back onto our bikes. The queen's chilling howls echoed from the amphitheater. I knew it was only a matter of time before she decided we would make a great appetizer.

As we raced down a row of festival booths, the sounds of that monstrosity faded into the distance. Charlie glanced back at the narrow lane behind us. "At least it's too big to squeeze down these paths," he said.

Directly to our right, the scorpion queen suddenly exploded through the Dunn Farms Jams booth. Her gargantuan body obliterated my mother's hard work like a wrecking ball. All that remained was a tangled ruin of broken wood and shredded fabric. Jam jars rained down around us, leaving smears of red and purple on the road as they smashed one by one.

There was no time to mourn the destruction of my mom's booth. Before the dust had even settled, the queen turned her eight hungry eyes toward us.

As she pursued us through the festival, she flattened everything in her path. Her tail whipped back and forth, batting objects in our direction. Without warning, a popcorn cart tumbled through the space between our bikes, then crashed in front of us. Glass and popcorn kernels scattered over the road.

"We can't outrun this thing forever!" Charlie shouted breathlessly.

He was right. She was gradually gaining on us. Charlie's face had grown red and sweaty, and I was in no better shape—we couldn't maintain this pace for much longer.

"If we can't outrun her, then maybe we can at least outmaneuver her!" I finally responded.

I took a sharp right-hand turn, then a left. We followed a zigzag path, taking so many random turns that after a while even *I* wasn't sure where we were in the maze.

When we could no longer hear the racket of the queen's trail of destruction, Charlie and I paused to catch our breath by the festival's carousel. It had gone dark and silent for the night. We got off our bikes and crouched down behind one of the plastic horses as we listened for any sign of the creature.

"Do you think we lost it?" I whispered when I heard nothing.

"The queen hatched five minutes ago," Charlie replied hopefully. "How smart could she possibly be?"

It was then I saw a shadow drift over Charlie's face.

I gazed up as a thorny tail rose over the curtain behind us.

28

The barb on the scorpion's tail split open and aimed straight at us. I could sense something bad was about to happen.

"Watch out!" I cried. I pushed Charlie out of the way, and then dove in the opposite direction.

From the end of the tail, a geyser of neon blue liquid sprayed through the space where we had been crouching a moment earlier. The substance coated a plastic horse on the carousel instead.

To my horror, the horse began to melt off its pole. Smoke rose off its mane in a cloud. In a matter of seconds, it formed a puddle on the carousel platform.

"Great, now it's spewing acid?" Charlie yelled as we scampered to the other side of the carousel. "What's next, breathing fire?"

"Don't jinx us!" I shouted back.

The queen started to stalk us around the carousel, but then she abruptly stopped. In the distance, the sounds of chatter and laughter echoed through the orchard.

It was coming from the town hall.

We had gotten so lost in the maze that we had inadvertently led her closer to the potluck supper.

Realizing that a much larger dinner awaited her elsewhere, the queen lost interest in us. She started to skitter in the direction of the celebration, where she would have access to a buffet of hundreds of townspeople.

Including my parents.

I would not let that happen. In a fit of desperation, I did the most insane thing I could think of:

I ran over to the row of burning jack-o'-lanterns that lined the nearest path.

I scooped one up.

And I hurled that pumpkin with all my might at the awful queen.

29

Direct hit. The pumpkin sailed across the distance between us and exploded against the creature's exoskeleton. She hissed as the fire licked at her shell.

"Get to the town hall," I ordered Charlie. "Warn everyone. I'll lure her in the opposite direction to buy you time."

"Kayla—" Charlie started to protest.

"Don't worry, I have an idea," I said.

With a reluctant nod, Charlie took off running in the direction of the potluck supper. Seconds later, he vanished completely into the mist.

The queen looked like she was considering chasing him, so I lobbed another jack-o'-lantern at her, then another. This time, her exoskeleton caught fire as the burning pumpkins exploded against her. She flopped onto her back, rolling in the dirt to put out the flames.

While the queen was trying to extinguish herself, I skirted around her to where my bike lay in the grass. I hurdled over one of her claws as it flailed around to slice me in two.

By the time she flipped back over, I was on my bike and racing through the dark orchard. A crazy plan had formed in my head, but for it to work, I needed her to follow me to the waterfall.

My whole body vibrated as the tires rumbled over the uneven ground. The queen's enraged howls reminded me that she was close behind.

Good. I was counting on that.

In the dense fog, it felt like the apple trees were closing in around me. One appeared through the mist right in my path, and I swerved sharply to avoid it.

My front tire snagged on a gnarled root. Next thing I knew, I was somersaulting over the handlebars.

I landed flat on my back, sending a cluster of rotting apples scattering around me like marbles. The air exploded out of my lungs. The bike flipped end over end beside me, nearly crushing my head in the process.

Somehow, through the dull ache in my back, I sucked in a deep breath and mustered the will to stand up. I abandoned the bike to finish the journey to the waterfall on foot. There were only two choices now:

Run or die.

By the time I reached the river, my lungs burned for air. I limped out onto the Cannonball's wooden platform, feeling it sway under the onslaught from the raging rapids below. The waterfall roared beneath me. One wrong step and the river would carry me right over the edge, to plummet a hundred feet to my death.

But what was waiting for me back the way that I came was so much more terrifying.

Before me, the giant jack-o'-lantern grinned menacingly. Flames danced in its eyes. *Abandon all hope*, the Cannonball seemed to be saying to me. *There is no escaping the beast.*

It was true. I had reached a dead end. I huddled in front of the pumpkin, shivering as the cold mist settled on my skin while I stared into the dark.

Over the deafening rush of water, I heard something else, a noise that made my stomach knot with dread.

The *click-click-click* of long, spindly legs, marching ominously toward me.

Through the dark fog, I watched the creature's eyes appear like eight sapphire flames.

Her slender, razor-sharp tail glinted above me, preparing to strike.

I remembered back to the first scorpion I had confronted at the old well, how its barbed stinger had gotten lodged in the bucket.

My idea had to work. It needed to work.

I bravely stood up in front of the Cannonball. Its firelight flickered around me.

I pounded my chest. "Come on!" I shouted at the beast. "Sting me already!"

I caught the telltale moment when the queen went totally still, the calm before the storm.

I dove out of the way just as her stinger plunged downward. One second later and it would have pierced my heart.

Instead, the barb speared through the Cannonball's thick rind. The queen tried to jerk her stinger free, but it had become trapped inside the giant pumpkin, which was almost as heavy as she was. She shrieked in panic as the fire inside began to roast her tail.

I knew it was only a matter of time before she

escaped. The queen was powerful, and any second now, she would wrestle her stinger free. I had to act quickly.

So I scrambled across the platform.

I wrapped my hand around the lever connected to the Cannonball's chute.

I took one last look at the queen. She froze and turned her glowing eyes to meet my gaze.

Then I pulled the lever.

The chute opened up and the Cannonball slid down into the river, dragging the queen along with it. She floundered hopelessly in the shallow water as the pumpkin stuck on her tail tugged her toward the waterfall's edge.

Right before she reached the falls, the queen's giant claw clamped down on a rock protruding from the water. For a few terrifying seconds, I feared she would escape her fate and chase me down to exact her revenge.

Then the weight of the Cannonball wrenched her claw free with a grating sound of bone against rock.

The rapids rushed her armored body forward the final few feet, until with a squawk, the queen vanished right over the edge.

I rushed to the railing to catch the final moment

of impact when the pumpkin and scorpion crashed into the basin far below with a magnificent splash.

When the foaming waters started to clear, chunks of pumpkin floated to the surface.

The queen never did. The water glowed blue with her blood.

I must have stood there for five minutes, fearing the scorpion would emerge from the basin. Finally, when I was sure I was safe, I collapsed with relief against the railing. The fog had begun to clear as quickly as it had descended on Orchard Falls, revealing the night sky above.

Eventually, I tilted my head up to the starry heavens and shouted a single triumphant word as loud as I could:

"Cannonball!"

"Hey, quit hogging the popcorn!" Yvonne said.

"It's *kettle* corn," Charlie corrected her. He grudgingly handed her the cavernous bowl.

The three of us sat on a picnic blanket in my backyard, surrounded by a smorgasbord of snacks. My dad had rigged a projector to play movies on a sheet draped against the back of the house. It was like having our own private drive-in theater.

Yvonne had been in charge of picking the film for our inaugural movie night. Charlie and I were immediately dismayed when she dropped her selection of DVDs onto the blanket.

"I couldn't decide between *Godzilla* and *Cloverfield*," she said. "At the last minute I thought: how about *Starship Troopers?*" She held up a cover that showed an enormous beetle attacking soldiers on a faraway planet.

Charlie and I exchanged uneasy glances. "Do you have any options that don't involve giant killer monsters or aliens?" I asked.

Yvonne squinted at me in confusion. "Why would you want to watch anything else?"

In the end, she grudgingly allowed me to pick a comedy from my own collection. As we watched and laughed, I could almost forget about the night of the Jack-o'-Lantern Festival a week ago.

Almost.

When Charlie had burst into the potluck supper that fateful evening and started screaming about a gigantic scorpion, everyone had gone quiet.

Then they started laughing at him.

Apparently, his reputation for trickery and pranks was widely known throughout Orchard Falls. By the time he had convinced his father to follow him, I had already vanquished the queen.

Even all the destruction at the festival couldn't get anyone to believe him. They just blamed all the flat-tened booths on a "microburst," some sort of freak windstorm.

The next day, when we climbed down to the

bottom of the waterfall, chunks of the giant jack-o'-lantern still floated in the basin.

The creature's exoskeleton was nowhere to be found. The water had washed away any trace of it, except for a smear of glowing blue blood on the rocks.

The shells of the two dead scorpions in the barn had vanished by the time I got back, as though they had simply crumbled to dust and drifted off with the wind.

As for the one we had locked in the silo, well—

"Who wants pie?" my mom's singsong voice interrupted my thoughts. "Fresh out of the oven!"

She had emerged from the back of the house holding a pie pan triumphantly above her head. The air over it rippled with heat waves.

When she placed it on our blanket, I recoiled. The pie was bright blue.

"Uh, Mom?" I said, suddenly alarmed. "What kind of pie is this exactly?"

She cocked her head to the side. "Pumpkin, obviously," she replied, as though it were the most ridiculous question she had ever heard.

"Then why is it blue?" Charlie asked, then added hopefully, "Food coloring?"

Mom grinned proudly and pointed uphill toward

where my pumpkin patch used to be. "I salvaged some of that smashed pumpkin. The shell was so big that I didn't want all your hard work to go to waste!"

"Looks delicious to me!" Yvonne exclaimed. She had cut herself a slice and was bringing a big fork full of blue pie up to her lips.

"Don't eat that!" Charlie shrieked at the same moment that I swatted the fork right out of her hands.

AFTER THE MOVIE WAS OVER, Yvonne's father picked her up first, and I walked Charlie to his bike. "You sure you don't want any help cleaning up all that food?" he asked, nodding back toward the picnic, where a mountain of leftover turkey burgers remained uneaten. My dad had been so excited that I'd made friends that he went overboard playing caterer for the movie night.

I waved a hand. "Nah, I'll take care of it."

Charlie smiled at me. It was hard to say if we would ever become close friends, but after the events a week ago, we shared a bond and a newfound respect for each other.

As he mounted his bike, he turned back to me.

"Hey, you never told me what happened to the fourth scorpion," he said. "You know, the one we locked in the silo."

I glanced back at the massive steel cylinder looming over the field. "It turned to ash like the rest of them. They all must have been linked to the queen, so that when she died, they did, too."

"I guess I was right about this place when I repainted your sign." Charlie grinned wickedly. "Welcome to Doom Farms!"

We both laughed as he pedaled off. He waved behind him as he cruised down the road.

As soon as he disappeared beyond the trees, I returned to the picnic blanket. I picked up the overflowing tray of sandwiches and wandered across the field to the silo.

With a deep breath, I opened a little flap in the door and slid the tray through.

I heard a rustling from inside, and then the sounds of sharp teeth gnashing at the mountain of burgers.

"Eat up," I whispered through the flap to the creature inside. A grin spread across my face. "I'm your queen now."

EPILOGUE

I nside his greenhouse, Dr. Umbra leaned over a hospital gurney. Through a pair of thick goggles, he examined what was left of the queen's carcass. The rushing water of Orchard Falls had swept away much of her organs and gooey entrails, until all that remained was a blue, mangled exoskeleton and a single enormous claw.

He almost didn't hear his assistant come up behind him. "I'm sorry," the woman in the white lab coat whispered. She had the same ageless, eerily smooth skin that he did. It was as though her scarlet hair had been pinned back so tightly that it pulled her face taut. "The queen really was quite beautiful in the fleeting time she was alive."

Dr. Umbra traced his gloved finger along the

sharp edge of the creature's pincers and sighed. "Such great potential gone to waste," he said. "Of all my creations, I think I loved her best." He took the goggles off his head and tossed them onto the gurney. "Oh well. No sense dwelling on the past when there is still so much work to be done. Will you walk with me to the Bonegarden?"

The assistant followed him through the greenhouse. They came to a pair of glass double doors, which whisked open when they approached. A dry, hot breeze blew over them as they stepped outside, churning up the blood red sand around them.

When the sandstorm finally cleared, they stood on the edge of a cliff, gazing out over a deep canyon. It looked like it had been scored into the earth with a skyscraper-sized knife. Giant bones protruded from the cliff tops surrounding it like broken fangs.

If you looked closely, you would realize that the canyon itself had formed inside the fossilized ribcage of a gargantuan skeleton.

Dr. Umbra could not help but smile as he looked out over the valley below. It glowed under the light of the three moons simmering on the horizon. Rows upon rows of colorful eggs stretched as far as the eye could see. Blue, red, green, violet, black—some were even colors the human eye could not process.

Pods of every shade concealing creatures of every nature.

Creatures of every nightmare.

His assistant watched a speckled yellow egg quiver and then go still. Soon it would hatch. "So what's our next move, father?" she asked.

Dr. Umbra considered this. "Contact the librarian," he replied finally.

"And what message should I deliver?"

A crack splintered through the yellow egg below. A single talon emerged.

"Tell him it's time to open the portal," Dr. Umbra said. Then he added:

"The big one."

ABOUT THE AUTHOR

Karsten Knight is known for writing books that feature mythologies from around the world. In 2011, Simon & Schuster Books for Young Readers published his debut, *Wildefire*, the first in a trilogy about a reincarnated Polynesian volcano goddess. Since then, he has authored the historical thriller *Nightingale, Sing* and the time-bending murder mystery *Patchwork*, and now channels his talent for terrifying readers into the *Bonegarden*.

Karsten studied creative writing at College of the Holy Cross and earned an MFA in writing for children from Simmons College. A lifelong resident of Massachusetts, he lives for fall New England weather —the perfect time of year for spooky stories.

For more information on Karsten and the *Bonegarden*, please visit www.karstenknightbooks.com.

Made in the USA
San Bernardino, CA
28 September 2018